Victor

Based on
The Railway Series
by the
Rev. W. Awdry

Illustrations by
Robin Davies
and **Jerry Smith**

EGMONT

EGMONT

We bring stories to life

First published in Great Britain in 2017
by Egmont UK Limited
The Yellow Building, 1 Nicholas Road, London W11 4AN

Thomas the Tank Engine & Friends™

CREATED BY BRITT ALLCROFT

HIT entertainment
ISBN 978 1 4052 8582 7
66570/1
Printed in Italy

Written by Emily Stead. Designed by Claire Yeo.
Series designed by Martin Aggett.

Egmont is passionate about helping to preserve the world's remaining ancient forests.
We only use paper from legal and sustainable forest sources.

This book is made from paper certified by the Forest Stewardship Council® (FSC®),
an organisation dedicated to promoting responsible management of forest resources.
For more information on the FSC, please visit www.fsc.org. To learn more about Egmont's
sustainable paper policy, please visit www.egmont.co.uk/ethical

FSC
MIX
Paper
FSC® C018306

Busy Victor runs the Sodor
Steamworks. All the engines like him!
When I was helping out one day,
it was Victor who showed me
that Really Useful Engines
always listen . . .

One day, Thomas had a special job. He had to look after the Steamworks while Victor was away.

"Victor will tell you what to do," The Fat Controller said. "So, listen carefully."

"Yes, Sir!" smiled Thomas. His firebox **fizzed** as he steamed away.

Everyone liked Victor. He knew how to fix engines big and small.

"Are you ready for a busy day?" Victor smiled, when Thomas arrived.

"I like being busy!" Thomas peeped happily.

"Listen carefully to what the engines say," Victor explained. "Kevin is here to help."

"That's right," chirped Kevin. "Ask me if you get in a fix!"

But Thomas was too excited to listen. He wanted to get on with his special job.

"Don't worry, Victor," he chuffed.

So Victor puffed away, leaving Thomas in charge.

Before long, Spencer arrived with a scratch on his paintwork. He was surprised to see Thomas.

"I'm in charge today," Thomas told Spencer. "I'll check you from whistle to wheels!"

Kevin was puzzled. "Spencer only has a scratch," he whispered.

But Thomas wouldn't listen. "Put Spencer on the hoist please, Kevin," he said.

Then Henry arrived, **spluttering** and **sneezing**.

"You've been given the wrong coal, Henry,"
Thomas told his friend.

"Oh no," Henry wheezed. "My problem is . . ."

But Thomas thought that he knew best, and
asked Kevin to fetch Henry's special coal.

Next, James puffed into the Steamworks.
His funnel was blocked with straw and twigs.

"You need a new funnel, James, and straight away!" Thomas said.

"No, Thomas . . ." James began.

But Thomas still wasn't listening. He told Kevin to find a spare funnel. Then he looked around the Steamworks, feeling proud.

Kevin's wheels wobbled. Thomas had given him too many jobs! He bumped backwards into the control panel, hoisting Spencer high in the air!

"Heaving hooks!" Kevin cried, dropping Henry's coal in surprise.

Black coal dust flew everywhere. The engines couldn't see a thing! Henry biffed James, who blew an enormous puff of steam.

Soon, the whole of the Steamworks was covered in soot and straw.

"Sizzling Sodor!" said a voice. "What has happened here?"

Victor had arrived back early!

Thomas looked at Victor, then at the **mess** and **muddle** all around.

"I'm sorry, Victor," Thomas said. "I was too excited. I didn't listen to Kevin, and I didn't listen to my friends. This **mess** is all my fault."

"You are right," huffed Victor. "But if you listen carefully now, we can fix everything together."

This time, Thomas did exactly as he was told.

First, they took Spencer down from the hoist.

"I only need my scratch painting," Spencer said.

"And I don't need more special coal — my firebox is making me **wheeze**," Henry puffed.

Thomas listened carefully. Then he fetched paint for Spencer, and helped to clean Henry's firebox.

"My funnel isn't broken," James told Thomas. "It just needs a clean and polish."

Before long, the Steamworks was **shining** and all the engines were fixed. They were ready to be Really Useful again.

Thomas was a wiser engine. "The next time I help out, I promise to listen!" he told Victor.

More about Victor

whistle

lamp

hand rail

hazard stripes

Victor's challenge to you

Look back through the pages of this book
and see if you can spot:

pigeon

twigs

paintbrush

funnel

sign

THE *THOMAS* ENGINE ADVENTURES

 Thomas

 Percy

 Harold

 James

 Cranky

 Spencer

 Gordon

 Flynn

 Toby

 Henry

 Hiro

 Emily

 Thomas and Bertie's Race

 Thomas Goes Crash!

 Kevin

 Diesel

 Troublesome Trucks

 Charlie

 The Thomas Way

 Thomas' New Friend

 Oliver

 Victor

 Thomas' Trusty Wheels

 Thomas Helps Hiro

EGMONT